TICKETS TO RIDE

BY MARK ROGALSKI

RUNNING PRESS
KIDS
PHILADELPHIA·LONDON

Library of Congress Control Number: 2005938632

ISBN-10: 0-7624-2782-5
ISBN-13: 978-0-7624-2782-6

This book may be ordered by mail from the publisher.
Please include $2.50 for postage and handling.
But try your bookstore first!

Published by Running Press Kids, an imprint of
Running Press Book Publishers
125 South Twenty-Second Street
Philadelphia, Pennsylvania 19103-4399

Visit us on the web!
www.runningpress.com

For Kellyanne

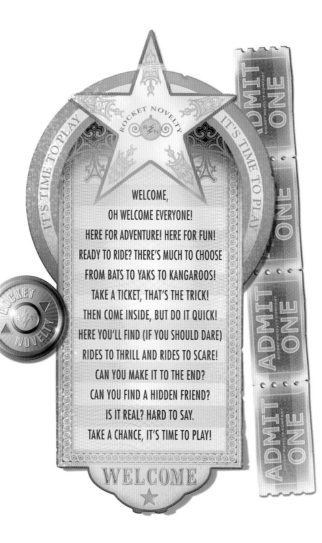

WELCOME,
OH WELCOME EVERYONE!
HERE FOR ADVENTURE! HERE FOR FUN!
READY TO RIDE? THERE'S MUCH TO CHOOSE
FROM BATS TO YAKS TO KANGAROOS!
TAKE A TICKET, THAT'S THE TRICK!
THEN COME INSIDE, BUT DO IT QUICK!
HERE YOU'LL FIND (IF YOU SHOULD DARE)
RIDES TO THRILL AND RIDES TO SCARE!
CAN YOU MAKE IT TO THE END?
CAN YOU FIND A HIDDEN FRIEND?
IS IT REAL? HARD TO SAY.
TAKE A CHANCE, IT'S TIME TO PLAY!

WELCOME

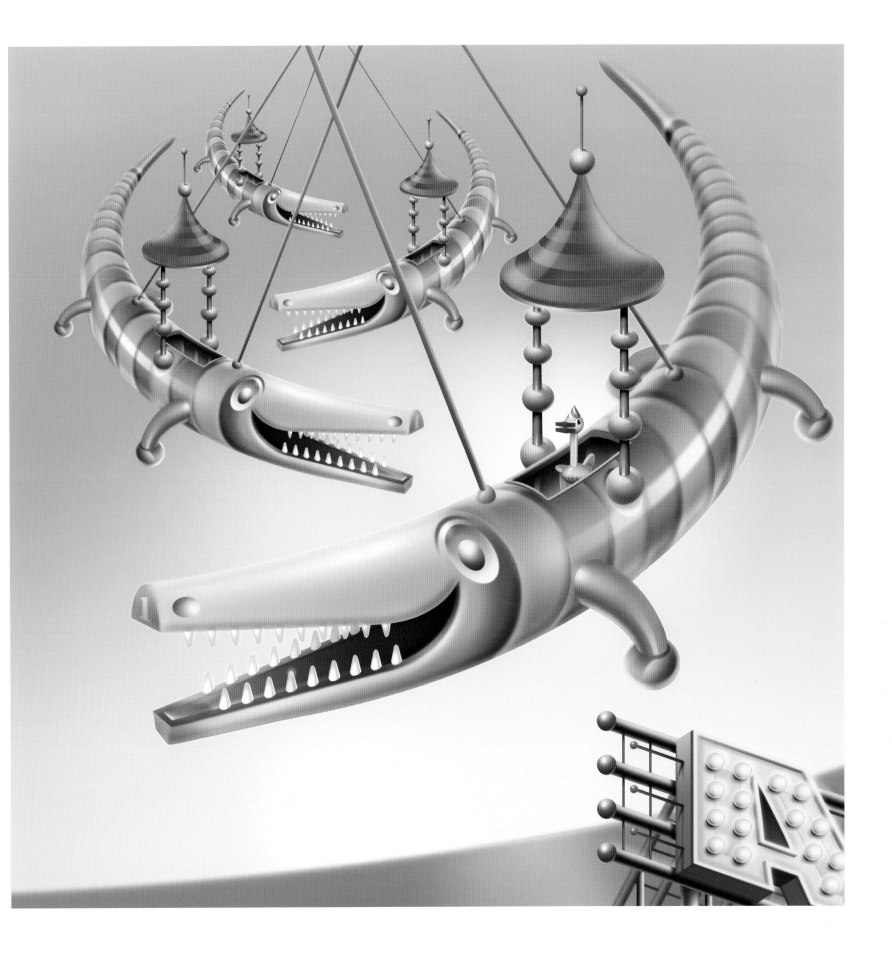

CAROUSEL CAMEL

THE CAROUSEL CAMEL
GOES ROUND AND ROUND.
TIME IS LOST
AND TIME IS FOUND.
GO BACKWARD, GROW YOUNGER,
GO FORWARD, GROW OLD.
GRAB THE BRASS RING
IF YOU FEEL SO BOLD!

BUT HEED THIS WARNING:
KEEP TIME ON TRACK.
IF YOU RIDE TOO LONG
YOU MAY NOT COME BACK!

003
Rocket Novelty Co.

FIRST PLACE

THE LUCKY DUCK DERBY

THE LUCKY DUCK DERBY
DOWN AT KNOCK KNOCK POND
SPURS ALL YOU PLUCKY DUCKS
TO GO ABOVE AND BEYOND!

THE CROWD WILL GET LOUD
AT THE STARTER DUCK'S QUACK
WHEN YOU SADDLE UP AND PADDLE
TO THE END AND THEN BACK!

BE THE FIRST TO FINISH
AND FIND FORTUNE COME YOUR WAY
AS THE LUCKIEST OF DUCKS
ON THIS DUCKY DERBY DAY!

ROCKET NOVELTY

4

LUCKY DUCK DERBY

1st
PLACE

1ST PLACE FINISH
LUCKY DUCK DERBY

KNOCK KNOCK POND
DERBY CHAMPION

Rocket Novelty Co.

ELEPHANT ED

ELEPHANT ED
HAS A FEZ ON HIS HEAD
AND A CASTLE
UPON HIS BACK!

EIGHTY FEET HIGH,
HE FILLS MOST OF THE SKY!
HE'S SO BIG THAT WE
CANNOT KEEP TRACK!

A HUNDRED YEARS OLD!
OR SO WE ARE TOLD.
WHAT MYSTERIES
HE MUST HIDE!

EPIC IN SIZE!
AS WIDE AS YOUR EYES!
THIS TICKET WILL
GET YOU INSIDE!

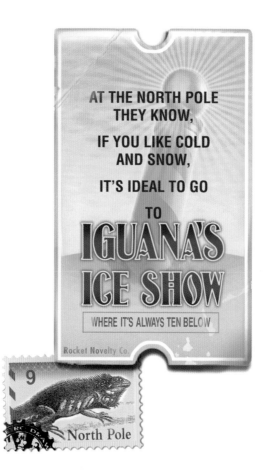

AT THE NORTH POLE
THEY KNOW,

IF YOU LIKE COLD
AND SNOW,

IT'S IDEAL TO GO

TO

IGUANA'S
ICE SHOW

WHERE IT'S ALWAYS TEN BELOW

Rocket Novelty Co.

9

North Pole

KING OF THE HILL

1938 • TRAIL GUIDE • 1939

◆◆ Kangar...
◆◆ Joey J...
◆◆ Flyer...
◆◆ Kabo...
◆◆ Pou...
◆◆ Rin...
◆◆ H...
◆◆ S...

◆◆◆◆

SKI JUMP CLUB 1947

WINTERLAND SKI PASS • 1962

SNOW PATROL 1953

Rocket Novelty Co.
presents a tale...

THAT'S
SOME KIND OF SLED,
KANGAROO FRED!

PLEASE RIDE WITH FRED –
HIS NOSE IS RED!

AND
YOU'RE DOING GREAT,
KANGAROO KATE!

GO RIDE WITH KATE –
HER POUCH HOLDS EIGHT!

BUT
KING OF THE HILL?
KANGAROO BILL!

COME RIDE WITH BILL –
AVOID THE CHILL!

the end

11

KEEP THIS TICKET STUB

**LION UP
AND LION DOWN!
LION LOOPING
ALL AROUND!**

LOOP the LOOP
LION

GOOD-BYE GROUND!
HELLO SKY!
HOLD YOUR CROWN!
HOLD YOUR TAIL!

NIGHT CRAWLER COASTER

In the garden of delight,
In the darkness of the night,
See the creepy-crawlies play
At the end of every day.

Spiders, biters, buzzers, itch.
Skeeters, stingers, which is which?

As fireflies all play 'til dawn,
Night Crawler Coaster creeps along!

Ride it now! Go ahead!
Before you have to go to bed!

ROCKET NOVELTY

OUR
OCTOPUS ORBITER BLAST
GOES FROM OCEAN TO OUTERSPACE FAST!
LIKE AN OLD-FASHIONED CYCLONE,
ONE SPINS THROUGH THE OZONE!
—BUT HURRY—
THIS OFFER WON'T LAST!

OFFER GOOD THRU OCTOBER

ONE FREE RIDE — LUCKY YOU!

15

rocket novelty

PARACHUTE PIGS

SIX-AND-A-HALF MILES
STRAIGHT UP IN THE SKY
ARE THE PARACHUTE PIGS!
–YES, THAT IS PRETTY HIGH–

PARACHUTE PIGS!
PARACHUTE PIGS!
LADIES AND GENTLEMEN,
HOLD ON TO YOUR WIGS!

DESPITE HOW IT LOOKS,
THESE PIGS REALLY CAN'T FLY.
BUT THEY CAN FLOAT ON AIR,
SO PLEASE GIVE THEM A TRY!

Pat. Pend., Phila., Penna. #16 Rocket Novelty

Little Queen Bee. She's so quiet. Here's a quarter. You should try it!

Little Queen Bee. Not so easy. Watch her stinger! Are you queasy?

TRAIN SCHED
FAIR WEATHER ROU

Well-paced, dependable s
1st Stop: Alligators in
2nd Stop: Bumper
3rd Stop: Care
4th Stop: Lucky

CLAIM
BAGGAGE ROOM
ROVELTY
NOVELTY
DESTINATION
Seat No. 19
Name

SCENIC RAILWAY

STEAMY THE SNAIL,
SLIDES DOWN THE RAIL.
ALL ABOARD FOR A SPECIAL TRIP.
PLANES CAN GET WAVY,
BOATS TAKE A NAVY.
ON THE ICE A SLED CAN SLIP.

STEAMY THE SNAIL

STEAMY THE SNAIL,
NEVER WILL FAIL,
GETTING YOU THERE FROM HERE!
HORSES ARE HAIRY,
SUBMARINES, SCARY.
BUT A SNAIL MAY TAKE A YEAR.

ROCKET NOVELTY

UNICORN
UMBRELLAS

Rocket Novelty Co.

UP, UP, AND AWAY,
TO UNCERTAIN HEIGHTS!
UMBRELLA BALLET!
SUCH UNCOMMON SIGHTS!

THE WINDS RUSH TO PLAY!
SKIES SING OF DELIGHTS!
A BEAUTIFUL DAY,
FOR UNICORN FLIGHTS!

021

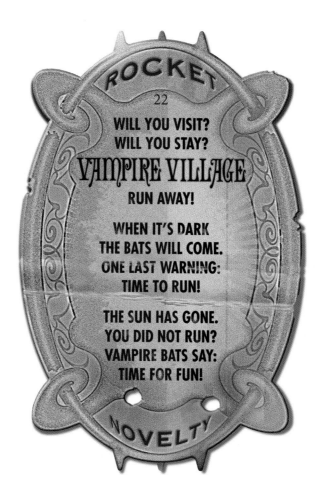

ROCKET

22

WILL YOU VISIT?
WILL YOU STAY?

VAMPIRE VILLAGE

RUN AWAY!

WHEN IT'S DARK
THE BATS WILL COME.
ONE LAST WARNING:
TIME TO RUN!

THE SUN HAS GONE.
YOU DID NOT RUN?
VAMPIRE BATS SAY:
TIME FOR FUN!

NOVELTY

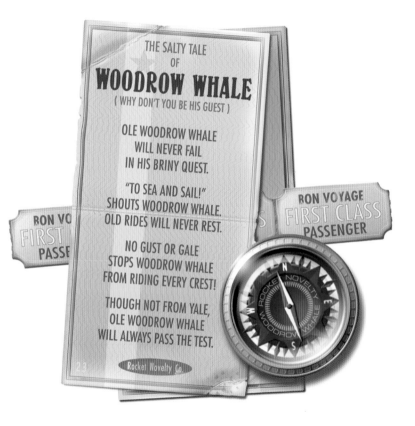

THE SALTY TALE
OF
WOODROW WHALE
(WHY DON'T YOU BE HIS GUEST)

OLE WOODROW WHALE
WILL NEVER FAIL
IN HIS BRINY QUEST.

"TO SEA AND SAIL!"
SHOUTS WOODROW WHALE.
OLD RIDES WILL NEVER REST.

NO GUST OR GALE
STOPS WOODROW WHALE
FROM RIDING EVERY CREST!

THOUGH NOT FROM YALE,
OLE WOODROW WHALE
WILL ALWAYS PASS THE TEST.

Rocket Novelty Co.

RON VOYAGE
FIRST CLASS
PASSENGER

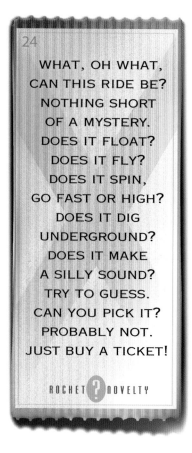

24

WHAT, OH WHAT,
CAN THIS RIDE BE?
NOTHING SHORT
OF A MYSTERY.
DOES IT FLOAT?
DOES IT FLY?
DOES IT SPIN,
GO FAST OR HIGH?
DOES IT DIG
UNDERGROUND?
DOES IT MAKE
A SILLY SOUND?
TRY TO GUESS.
CAN YOU PICK IT?
PROBABLY NOT.
JUST BUY A TICKET!

ROCHET ? NOVELTY

Rocket Novelty Co

All ducks quack.
Cows moo back.
Mules just pack.
The Yak Kayak!

The Yak Kayak

It's Your Turn!

Rocket Novelty Co

Pancake stack.
Midnight snack.
Dental plaque.
Oh, Yak Kayak!

Oh, Yak Kayak

It's Your Turn!

Rocket Novelty Co

Knuckles crack.
Toes tic-tac.
Jumping jack.
Yell Yak Kayak!

Yell Yak Kayak

It's Your Turn!

ACK
YAK

In Funny Business since 1925

ZEBRA ZEPPELIN

IS THAT A ZEBRA
OVERHEAD?
HOP ON BOARD OR
GO TO BED!

TAKE A CHANCE,
IT'S TIME TO GO!
STAY IN BED,
YOU'LL NEVER KNOW!

MAKE SOME NOISE!
LAUGH AND SCREAM!
SO MUCH FUN,
MUST BE A DREAM!

SO MUCH FUN ~ IS IT A DREAM?

TICKET TO RIDE

ZZZ'S PLEASE   Rocket Novelty

Monkey Island

Coconut Cove

Wishbone Beach

WINTERLAND

Knock
Knock
Pond

ENTER HERE!

THE *Legend* OF

DIZZYLAND

DREAM PARK

- ········ LOST & FOUND
- ········ SAFE & SOUND
- ···· BATHROOM BREAKS
- ···· BEWARE OF SNAKES
- ········ FRESH FISH
- ········ MAKE A WISH
- ······ ICE CREAM TREAT
- ········ HAVE A SEAT
- ········ FALLING PIGS
- ···· CROWNS AND WIGS
- ········ RED BALLOON
- ········ FROG LAGOON
- ········ SECRET WAY
- ········ TIME TO PLAY

HOPE YOU ALL ENJOY YOUR STAY!

ROCKET NOVELTY

TICKETS TO RIDE

Within the images of each ride
two special items cleverly hide:
a number (one through twenty-six),
and a duck with lots of tricks.
Try to find them if you can.
Just go through the park again!

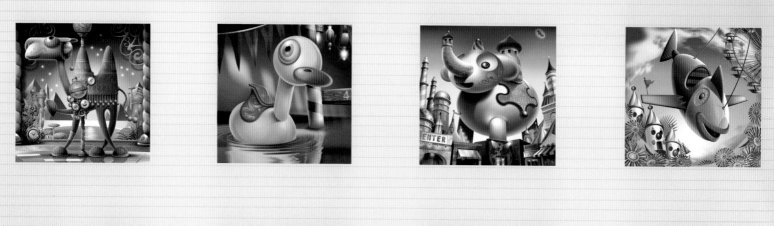